# CONTENTS

# WHAT CAN ASTROLOGY
## *do for me?*

Astrology is a powerful tool for self-awareness. The idea that we are all connected—that the shifting energies of the Sun, Moon, and planets above affect us here on Earth—is an ancient and philosophical belief. Astrology isn't fortune-telling—it can't predict your future and it doesn't deal in absolutes. It simply says that you are part of the universe around you, and by studying the stars, it's possible to learn more about yourself.

Why is this so important? Because the better understanding you have of your own inner makeup—your skills, your talents, your needs, and your fears—the more insight you gain into why you act the way you do. And this gives you choices, empowering you to make changes and to build on your strengths. It makes it easier to feel confident and to accept yourself, quirks and all.

There are countless daily horoscopes in newspapers, magazines, and online. But this book looks at more than just your star sign, which is only a small part of your personality picture. It helps you to find your Rising sign, which was appearing over the Eastern horizon at the time of your birth, and has a lot to tell you about the way others see you. You can also work out your Moon sign, which reveals the real you deep down inside, giving you the chance to get to grips with your innermost emotions, desires, fears, and obsessions.

With a clearer picture of who you are, life becomes less complicated. Instead of trying to live up to others' expectations and being someone you're not, you can work instead on becoming the best version of yourself possible—someone who understands their talents and needs, who is perfectly unique, and is happy.

# What is
# ASTROLOGY?

The stars and planets have always inspired a sense of wonder. The ancient peoples of Babylonia, Persia, Egypt, Greece, and India were all fascinated by the cycles of the Moon, the rising and setting of the Sun, the position of the constellations, and what it all meant. As these civilizations developed, they connected what they saw in the sky with the people and events on Earth, and astrology was born.

In ancient times, astrology was used to help monarchs rule. Kings and emperors would employ astrologers to predict the weather, speak to the gods, and help manage the country.

Modern astrology has evolved to help ordinary people like you and me understand ourselves better—how we behave, how we feel about each other, and how we can make the best of who we are.

# THE SIGNS OF THE ZODIAC

Today we know that the planets revolve around the Sun, but astrology is based on how we see the solar system from here on Earth. The Zodiac is a group of 12 constellations that, from our viewpoint, seem to rotate around Earth over the course of a year, like a huge wheel. These constellations are named for the animals and objects that our ancestors thought they looked most like—the ram, the lion, the scorpion, and so on. Your Sun sign tells you which of the constellations the Sun was moving through on the day you were born. The signs have a natural order that never varies, beginning with Aries. The dates given on the right change slightly from year to year for the same reasons we have a leap year—each of our days is slightly longer than 24 hours. If you were born at the beginning or end of a sign, called "the cusp," it's worth checking your Sun sign online to be sure.

| ARIES | LIBRA |
|:---:|:---:|
| March 21–April 20 | September 23–October 22 |
| TAURUS | SCORPIO |
| April 21–May 21 | October 23–November 21 |
| GEMINI | SAGITTARIUS |
| May 22–June 21 | November 22–December 21 |
| CANCER | CAPRICORN |
| June 22–July 22 | December 22–January 20 |
| LEO | AQUARIUS |
| July 23–August 23 | January 21–February 19 |
| VIRGO | PISCES |
| August 24–September 22 | February 20–March 20 |

# THE FOUR ELEMENTS

*Each Sun sign is associated with one of four elements—*
*Fire, Earth, Air, and Water.*

### FIRE

**Aries, Leo, Sagittarius**
*Fire signs are passionate, dynamic, and temperamental.*
**They mix well with**: Fire and Air types

### EARTH

**Taurus, Virgo, Capricorn**
*Earth signs are practical, cautious, and reliable.*
**They mix well with**: Water and Earth types

### AIR

**Aquarius, Gemini, Libra**
*Air signs are quick, curious, and adventurous.*
**They mix well with**: Air and Fire types

### WATER

**Pisces, Cancer, Scorpio**
*Water signs are sensitive, emotional, and kind.*
**They mix well with**: Earth and Water types

# THE PLANETS

Astrology looks at the positions of the stars and planets at the time and place of your birth. The Sun and Moon aren't technically planets, but they're referred to that way by astrologers for ease of use. The Sun is a great place to start—it's the most important object in the solar system. Your Sun sign describes the essence of your identity and says a great deal about your potential—the person you might become.

The position the Moon held in the sky at the time of your birth has a strong influence, too. It describes your emotions—how you feel deep inside. It can give you a better understanding of what you need to feel loved and cared for.

And there's also your Rising sign. This is the sign of the Zodiac that was appearing over the Eastern horizon at the time of your birth. It tells you more about how you interact with the world around you, especially to new situations. It's the filter through which you perceive the world and the impression you give to others on first meeting. Which means it's also how others often see you.

The positions of the other planets—Venus, Mercury, Mars, etc.—in your birth chart all have their own effect. But these three taken together—Sun, Moon, and Rising sign—will give you a deeper understanding of who you are and what you could become, your strengths and weaknesses, your real self.

# Your SUN sign

# SAGITTARIUS

November 22–December 21

**SYMBOL**
The Archer

**ELEMENT**
Fire

**RULING PLANET**
Jupiter

**BIRTHSTONE**
Turquoise

**COLOR**
Purple

**BODY PART**
Hips, thighs

**DAY OF THE WEEK**
Thursday

**FLOWER**
Carnation

**CHARACTER TRAITS**
Adventurous, optimistic, lucky

**KEY PHRASE**
"I seek"

# YOUR SUN SIGN

When people talk about astrology and ask about your star sign, they're referring to your Sun sign. It tells you which of the 12 constellations of the Zodiac the Sun was moving through on the day you were born. This makes it easy to work out, which is one of the reasons for its popularity. If you'd like to know the Sun sign of a friend or family member, the table on page 7 shows which days the Sun occupies each of the signs over the course of a year.

The Sun is the heart of your chart—it's the essence of who you are and symbolizes the potential of what you can achieve. It's important to remember, though, that it is only a part of the whole picture when it comes to astrology. It's a wonderful starting point, but there are many other layers encasing your core identity, all of which affect the inner you.

## ALL ABOUT YOU

Born with the Sun in Sagittarius, your energy and love of learning gives you the potential to widen people's experience, giving them a fresh perspective.

You're a carefree soul and, ruled by Jupiter, lady luck always seems to be smiling down upon you. Your relentless optimism and curious mind creates your own good fortune, too.

Your friends are important to you so long as they don't try to tell you what to do—you like to feel free. This means you're not one to follow the crowd and prefer to do things your own way.

Some of your friends may even feel a little jealous of you now and then—everything always seems to fall into place so easily for you. But any negativity is quickly forgotten the next time they hang out with you—your love of adventure and willingness to try new things means there's always something exciting around the corner.

You're popular in your circle because you aren't selfish with your belongings. If there's a party coming up, your friends will want to get ready at your place—they know you won't mind them raiding your wardrobe.

And guess what? You might even be able to "read" your friends. As a Sagittarian, you find it super-easy to tune into other people's wavelengths and can often work out what those closest to you are thinking—even before they do!

## Likes

To move
Like-minded people
Taking risks
Animals
Freedom
Adventure

## Dislikes

Alone-time
Showing emotion
Being bossed around
FOMO

## HOW TO BRING OUT YOUR BEST

You just love to explore. As you get older, you'll grab the chance to jet off to new places at every opportunity. You're probably always begging your parents to let you go on the latest school trip: it feeds your desire to find out as much as you can about the world. So, you're happiest with like-minded buddies who are just as eager to pack a bag and head off on an adventure as you are.

You also have a knack for making people feel as though they can tell you anything; it's a precious gift to have. Occasionally your enthusiasm does get the better of you, though, and you blurt out what's on your mind without thinking. Remember to take a moment to think things through—it'll save you from those awkward situations.

Your independent streak is a great asset, although sometimes it can make you feel invincible even though asking for help is more sensible. It takes strength to admit you might need a hand from time to time, plus it builds stronger bonds with the important people in your life.

## Strengths

Relaxed
Open-minded
Spontaneous
Visionary
Competitive
Knowledgeable
Thick-skinned

## Weaknesses

Opinionated
Headstrong
Irresponsible
Impatient

## SECRET FEARS

You're scared of not living life to the full, so you often struggle with everyday chores. Well, they're just so boring, aren't they? And a bored Sagittarian is an unhappy one. See if you can find new ways to inject some much-needed fun into those dull routines.

With the archer as your symbol, you don't like to miss any targets you're reaching for. It can make you feel like you've failed. Try not to look backward and waste precious time. Especially as patience isn't a quality you possess in abundance— if things suddenly grind to a halt, you worry your carefully laid plans will be derailed. Remember that temporary setbacks are a part of life. You're so used to looking on the bright side, it shouldn't be too hard.

### Most likely to . . .

Travel

Speak your mind

See the bigger picture

Be an athlete

Say "I'm not arguing, I'm just explaining why I'm right"

Not care what others think

Help at an animal shelter

# Your RISING sign

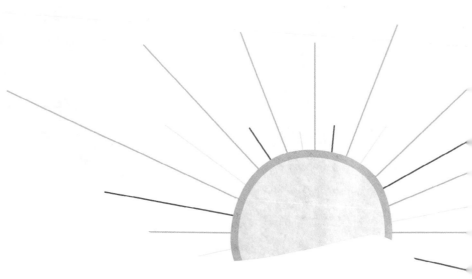

# YOUR RISING SIGN

Your Rising sign, also known as your Ascendant, is the sign that was rising over the Eastern horizon (the place where the Sun rises each day) when you were born. It describes how you see the world and the people around you and how they see you—the first impression that you give and receive, the image you project, and the initial reaction you might have to a new situation. A person with Leo Rising, for example, may strike you as warm and engaging, whereas Pisces Rising is more sensitive and possibly shy. Because the Ascendant is determined by the exact time and place you were born, it is the most personal point in your chart. Many astrologers believe this makes it just as important as your Sun sign.

## HOW TO FIND YOUR ASCENDANT

This is where it gets a bit tricky. There's a reason that popular astrology only deals with your Sun sign—your Rising sign can be more difficult to work out. But don't be put off. If you know your Sun sign and your time of birth, you can use the table on the right to give you a good idea. To be totally accurate you do need to take into account factors like time zone and daylight savings, and there are plenty of free online calculators that will do just that.

## YOUR HOUR OF BIRTH

| YOUR SUN SIGN | 6:00 AM to 8:00 AM | 8:00 AM to 10:00 AM | 10:00 AM to 12:00 PM | 12:00 PM to 2:00 PM | 2:00 PM to 4:00 PM | 4:00 PM to 6:00 PM | 6:00 PM to 8:00 PM | 8:00 PM to 10:00 PM | 10:00 PM to 12:00 AM | 12:00 AM to 2:00 AM | 2:00 AM to 4:00 AM | 4:00 AM to 6:00 AM |
|---|---|---|---|---|---|---|---|---|---|---|---|---|
| **ARIES** ♈ | ♉ | ♊ | ♋ | ♌ | ♍ | ♎ | ♏ | ♐ | ♑ | ♒ | ♓ | ♈ |
| **TAURUS** ♉ | ♊ | ♋ | ♌ | ♍ | ♎ | ♏ | ♐ | ♑ | ♒ | ♓ | ♈ | ♉ |
| **GEMINI** ♊ | ♋ | ♌ | ♍ | ♎ | ♏ | ♐ | ♑ | ♒ | ♓ | ♈ | ♉ | ♊ |
| **CANCER** ♋ | ♌ | ♍ | ♎ | ♏ | ♐ | ♑ | ♒ | ♓ | ♈ | ♉ | ♊ | ♋ |
| **LEO** ♌ | ♍ | ♎ | ♏ | ♐ | ♑ | ♒ | ♓ | ♈ | ♉ | ♊ | ♋ | ♌ |
| **VIRGO** ♍ | ♎ | ♏ | ♐ | ♑ | ♒ | ♓ | ♈ | ♉ | ♊ | ♋ | ♌ | ♍ |
| **LIBRA** ♎ | ♏ | ♐ | ♑ | ♒ | ♓ | ♈ | ♉ | ♊ | ♋ | ♌ | ♍ | ♎ |
| **SCORPIO** ♏ | ♐ | ♑ | ♒ | ♓ | ♈ | ♉ | ♊ | ♋ | ♌ | ♍ | ♎ | ♏ |
| **SAGITTARIUS** ♐ | ♑ | ♒ | ♓ | ♈ | ♉ | ♊ | ♋ | ♌ | ♍ | ♎ | ♏ | ♐ |
| **CAPRICORN** ♑ | ♒ | ♓ | ♈ | ♉ | ♊ | ♋ | ♌ | ♍ | ♎ | ♏ | ♐ | ♑ |
| **AQUARIUS** ♒ | ♓ | ♈ | ♉ | ♊ | ♋ | ♌ | ♍ | ♎ | ♏ | ♐ | ♑ | ♒ |
| **PISCES** ♓ | ♈ | ♉ | ♊ | ♋ | ♌ | ♍ | ♎ | ♏ | ♐ | ♑ | ♒ | ♓ |

# WHAT YOUR RISING SIGN SAYS ABOUT YOU

*Once you have figured out your Ascendant, you are ready to discover more about how you see the world, and how it sees you.*

### ARIES RISING

The influence of physically active Aries means that you can find yourself racing through the day, hardly giving yourself time to sit down. You might feel guilty for taking a break, but it's important to encourage yourself to kick back and relax in order to stay happy and healthy. Despite a tendency to spread yourself too thinly—and turn up late for dates and appointments—people can't help but warm to your infectious energy and optimism.

### TAURUS RISING

Taurus delivers a dose of down-to-earth practicality to help you turn your Sagittarian idealism into reality. You love a challenging debate, but sometimes the bull's stubbornness can get the better of you. While this doesn't faze your close friends (they're probably used to it and tease you about it), it can cause problems with other people. In love, you're charming, but you like to feel that your partner belongs to you. Learning to relax and trust that things will be okay will help you to overcome this quirk.

### GEMINI RISING

Gemini's highly sociable nature perfectly complements the Sagittarian lust for life. You have a chameleon-like ability to adapt to most settings you find yourself in, and your genuine openness and optimism quickly wins you friends. You can be quite the chatterbox, which people usually find endearing. However, although your tendency to wing it works 90 percent of the time, it might be an idea to apply yourself more seriously where life's important stuff is concerned. Do this and the sky's the limit.

### CANCER RISING

The Cancerian influence helps to rein in your Sagittarian fondness for chasing fun at the cost of more mundane commitments in your life. In fact, it can transform you into one of the Zodiac's hardest-working signs, firing you up with a willingness to do whatever it takes to get the desired result. You have a lovely way about you, a gentle, authentic energy, which attracts other kind souls toward you. Your intuition helps you develop powerful insights into other people.

### LEO RISING

As you would imagine, when two Fire signs come together, the results can be explosive. You tend to rush in where angels fear to tread. Although you're the life of the party, you might notice that people who are hanging on your every word one minute are gone the next. It's possible that they feel overwhelmed by your full-on energy. However, you're warm, flexible, and open to different opinions. You're a natural-born leader and can use your dazzling charm to inspire people.

### VIRGO RISING

The Virgoan influence acts as a pause button, helping you to stop and think before you jump in with that customary Sagittarian abandon. You usually read the small print of a situation more carefully, so you can make more informed choices. You have a refreshing live-and-let-live attitude to life, which gathers a wonderfully diverse mix of friends around you. They feel free to be their most authentic self and, in turn, so do you. Surprisingly, despite your confident attitude, you've no desire to grab the limelight.

### LIBRA RISING

If left unchecked, your supreme confidence can be intimidating, but adding a touch of Libra's thoughtfulness into the mix softens this aspect. You're outspoken and deeply curious about the world. When it comes to friendships, you're high on the popularity list. You're a sociable creature, you seek out the best in people, and you have a kind, forgiving nature. Be careful not to be taken in too easily by those who aren't so deserving of your affections.

### SCORPIO RISING

Blending Scorpio into the Sagittarian mix is a little like adding rocket boosters to your already energetic approach to life. You're never in one place for very long, and your friends and family sometimes have trouble tracking you down. You might be in danger of biting off more than you can chew, which can lead to letting people down. Take a second to think if you can really add another commitment to your packed schedule. You absorb information super-quickly and love to give your brain a workout.

### SAGITTARIUS RISING

You are the explorer of the Zodiac. Sagittarius doubled means you're often on the lookout for all kinds of adventure. As a free spirit, you're hungry to learn about new cultures, and you make friends wherever you roam. You're open to everyone and everything around you, and you enjoy talking to people and learning about their lives and dreams. Your spontaneity might lead to mistakes, but you're sincere, you like to help others, and you have a strong sense of right and wrong.

### CAPRICORN RISING

The strict planet of Saturn rules Capricorn, sometimes bringing with it a stern element to your personality. However, your sweet and positive Sagittarius nature brings lightness to most situations. Although you're not one for blurting out your feelings at the drop of a hat, you have a big heart, and you're a real softy when it comes to animals and children. You're ambitious and usually know what it takes to achieve your goals. You have an expansive view of the world and tend to think big.

### AQUARIUS RISING

Air and Fire get on like nobody's business, and this is no exception. You're probably an expert at talking things through calmly to reach a happy outcome. Your charm encourages others to get on board with projects you have ready to go, and you excel at bringing people together. While you're open-minded, tolerant, and a good communicator, you're also an idealist, whose fiery side might show itself when you're defending your principles.

### PISCES RISING

With its caring, kindhearted nature, Pisces brings a softness to Sagittarius. A challenge you might experience is learning to walk the line between keeping the peace without sacrificing your own beliefs. If you can stay calm and focused, however, you'll achieve this. You're inspired to create beauty, and this might play a part in your future career choices. While you're ambitious, you often need the encouragement of others to give you the determination you need to succeed.

# Your MOON sign

# YOUR MOON SIGN

The Moon rules your emotions and your inner moods, telling you what you need to feel safe, comfortable, and loved. Knowing your Moon sign should give you a more complete picture of your unique self, helping you to express needs you might be struggling to understand. Suppose your Sun sign is Aries but being first has never been important to you—a Moon in Virgo may be telling you to hang back and fade into the background. Or you might have the Sun in home-loving Cancer but feel an urge to get out there and see the world. Perhaps that's because your Moon is in freedom-loving Aquarius.

## HOW TO FIND YOUR MOON SIGN

Just like your Rising sign, finding your Moon sign is more complicated than finding your Sun sign. That's because the Moon seems to move so quickly, taking just about a month to pass through all of the constellations. Thankfully, the tables on the right and on the next page make finding it a simple process.

First, find your year of birth. Then locate your birth month at the top of the table. Find your date of birth in the column below it, and this will give you your Moon sign. If your date of birth isn't listed, the one before it is your Moon sign.

*For example, suppose your date of birth is March 4, 1995. The date before this is March 2, for which the Moon sign is Aries. This would mean your Moon sign is Aries.*

| JAN | FEB | MAR | APR | MAY | JUN | JUL | AUG | SEP | OCT | NOV | DEC |
|-----|-----|-----|-----|-----|-----|-----|-----|-----|-----|-----|-----|

### BORN IN THE YEAR 1995

| JAN | FEB | MAR | APR | MAY | JUN | JUL | AUG | SEP | OCT | NOV | DEC |
|-----|-----|-----|-----|-----|-----|-----|-----|-----|-----|-----|-----|
| 2 Aqu | 1 Pis | 2 Ari | 1 Tau | 1 Gem | 2 Leo | 2 Vir | 3 Sco | 1 Sag | 2 Aqu | 1 Pis | 3 Tau |
| 4 Pis | 3 Ari | 5 Tau | 3 Gem | 3 Can | 5 Vir | 4 Lib | 5 Sag | 3 Cap | 5 Pis | 3 Ari | 5 Gem |
| 7 Ari | 5 Tau | 7 Gem | 6 Can | 6 Leo | 7 Lib | 6 Sco | 7 Cap | 5 Aqu | 7 Ari | 5 Tau | 8 Can |
| 9 Tau | 8 Gem | 10 Can | 9 Leo | 8 Vir | 9 Sco | 8 Sag | 9 Aqu | 7 Pis | 9 Tau | 8 Gem | 10 Leo |
| 12 Gem | 10 Can | 12 Leo | 11 Vir | 10 Lib | 11 Sag | 10 Cap | 11 Pis | 9 Ari | 12 Gem | 10 Can | 13 Vir |
| 14 Can | 13 Leo | 14 Vir | 13 Lib | 13 Sco | 13 Cap | 12 Aqu | 13 Ari | 12 Tau | 14 Can | 13 Leo | 15 Lib |
| 16 Leo | 15 Vir | 17 Lib | 15 Sco | 15 Sag | 15 Aqu | 14 Pis | 15 Tau | 14 Gem | 17 Leo | 15 Vir | 17 Sco |
| 19 Vir | 17 Lib | 19 Sco | 17 Sag | 17 Cap | 17 Pis | 16 Ari | 18 Gem | 17 Can | 19 Vir | 18 Lib | 19 Sag |
| 21 Lib | 19 Sco | 21 Sag | 19 Cap | 19 Aqu | 19 Ari | 19 Tau | 20 Can | 19 Leo | 21 Lib | 20 Sco | 21 Cap |
| 23 Sco | 22 Sag | 23 Cap | 21 Aqu | 21 Pis | 22 Tau | 22 Gem | 23 Leo | 22 Vir | 23 Sco | 22 Sag | 23 Aqu |
| 25 Sag | 24 Cap | 25 Aqu | 24 Pis | 23 Ari | 24 Gem | 24 Can | 25 Vir | 24 Lib | 26 Sag | 24 Cap | 25 Pis |
| 27 Cap | 26 Aqu | 27 Pis | 26 Ari | 26 Tau | 27 Can | 27 Leo | 28 Lib | 26 Sco | 28 Cap | 26 Aqu | 28 Ari |
| 30 Aqu | 28 Pis | 30 Ari | 28 Tau | 28 Gem | 29 Leo | 29 Vir | 30 Sco | 28 Sag | 30 Aqu | 28 Pis | 30 Tau |
|  |  |  |  | 31 Can |  | 31 Lib |  | 30 Cap |  | 30 Ari |  |

### BORN IN THE YEAR 1996

| JAN | FEB | MAR | APR | MAY | JUN | JUL | AUG | SEP | OCT | NOV | DEC |
|-----|-----|-----|-----|-----|-----|-----|-----|-----|-----|-----|-----|
| 1 Gem | 3 Leo | 1 Leo | 2 Lib | 2 Sco | 2 Cap | 2 Aqu | 2 Ari | 1 Tau | 3 Can | 2 Leo | 2 Vir |
| 4 Can | 5 Vir | 3 Vir | 4 Sco | 4 Sag | 4 Aqu | 4 Pis | 4 Tau | 3 Gem | 5 Leo | 4 Vir | 4 Lib |
| 6 Leo | 8 Lib | 6 Lib | 7 Sag | 6 Cap | 6 Pis | 6 Ari | 7 Gem | 6 Can | 8 Vir | 7 Lib | 6 Sco |
| 9 Vir | 10 Sco | 8 Sco | 9 Cap | 8 Aqu | 9 Ari | 8 Tau | 9 Can | 8 Leo | 10 Lib | 9 Sco | 9 Sag |
| 11 Lib | 12 Sag | 10 Sag | 11 Aqu | 10 Pis | 11 Tau | 11 Gem | 12 Leo | 11 Vir | 13 Sco | 11 Sag | 11 Cap |
| 14 Sco | 14 Cap | 13 Cap | 13 Pis | 12 Ari | 13 Gem | 13 Can | 14 Vir | 13 Lib | 15 Sag | 13 Cap | 13 Aqu |
| 16 Sag | 16 Aqu | 15 Aqu | 15 Ari | 15 Tau | 16 Can | 16 Leo | 17 Lib | 15 Sco | 17 Cap | 16 Aqu | 15 Pis |
| 18 Cap | 18 Pis | 17 Pis | 17 Tau | 17 Gem | 18 Leo | 18 Vir | 19 Sco | 18 Sag | 19 Aqu | 18 Pis | 17 Ari |
| 20 Aqu | 20 Ari | 19 Ari | 20 Gem | 19 Can | 21 Vir | 21 Lib | 21 Sag | 20 Cap | 21 Pis | 20 Ari | 19 Tau |
| 22 Pis | 23 Tau | 21 Tau | 22 Can | 22 Leo | 23 Lib | 23 Sco | 24 Cap | 22 Aqu | 23 Ari | 22 Tau | 22 Gem |
| 24 Ari | 25 Gem | 23 Gem | 25 Leo | 25 Vir | 26 Sco | 25 Sag | 26 Aqu | 24 Pis | 26 Tau | 24 Gem | 24 Can |
| 26 Tau | 27 Can | 26 Can | 27 Vir | 27 Lib | 28 Sag | 27 Cap | 28 Pis | 26 Ari | 28 Gem | 27 Can | 26 Leo |
| 29 Gem |  | 28 Leo | 30 Lib | 29 Sco | 30 Cap | 29 Aqu | 30 Ari | 28 Tau | 30 Can | 29 Leo | 29 Vir |
| 31 Can |  | 31 Vir |  | 31 Sag |  | 31 Pis |  | 30 Gem |  |  | 31 Lib |

### BORN IN THE YEAR 1997

| JAN | FEB | MAR | APR | MAY | JUN | JUL | AUG | SEP | OCT | NOV | DEC |
|-----|-----|-----|-----|-----|-----|-----|-----|-----|-----|-----|-----|
| 3 Sco | 1 Sag | 1 Sag | 1 Aqu | 1 Pis | 1 Tau | 1 Gem | 2 Leo | 3 Lib | 3 Sco | 1 Sag | 1 Cap |
| 5 Sag | 4 Cap | 3 Cap | 4 Pis | 3 Ari | 4 Gem | 3 Can | 4 Vir | 6 Sco | 5 Sag | 4 Cap | 3 Aqu |
| 7 Cap | 6 Aqu | 5 Aqu | 6 Ari | 5 Tau | 6 Can | 5 Leo | 7 Lib | 8 Sag | 8 Cap | 6 Aqu | 5 Pis |
| 9 Aqu | 8 Pis | 7 Pis | 8 Tau | 7 Gem | 8 Leo | 8 Vir | 9 Sco | 10 Cap | 10 Aqu | 8 Pis | 8 Ari |
| 11 Pis | 10 Ari | 9 Ari | 10 Gem | 9 Can | 11 Vir | 10 Lib | 12 Sag | 12 Aqu | 12 Pis | 10 Ari | 10 Tau |
| 13 Ari | 12 Tau | 11 Tau | 12 Can | 12 Leo | 13 Lib | 13 Sco | 14 Cap | 15 Pis | 14 Ari | 12 Tau | 12 Gem |
| 15 Tau | 14 Gem | 13 Gem | 14 Leo | 14 Vir | 16 Sco | 15 Sag | 16 Aqu | 17 Ari | 16 Tau | 14 Gem | 14 Can |
| 18 Gem | 16 Can | 16 Can | 17 Vir | 17 Lib | 18 Sag | 18 Cap | 18 Pis | 19 Tau | 18 Gem | 17 Can | 16 Leo |
| 20 Can | 19 Leo | 18 Leo | 19 Lib | 19 Sco | 20 Cap | 20 Aqu | 21 Ari | 21 Gem | 20 Can | 19 Leo | 19 Vir |
| 23 Leo | 21 Vir | 21 Vir | 22 Sco | 22 Sag | 22 Aqu | 22 Pis | 22 Tau | 23 Can | 23 Leo | 21 Vir | 21 Lib |
| 25 Vir | 24 Lib | 23 Lib | 24 Sag | 24 Cap | 24 Pis | 24 Ari | 24 Gem | 25 Leo | 25 Vir | 24 Lib | 24 Sco |
| 28 Lib | 26 Sco | 26 Sco | 27 Cap | 26 Aqu | 26 Ari | 26 Tau | 27 Can | 28 Vir | 28 Lib | 26 Sco | 26 Sag |
| 30 Sco |  | 28 Sag | 29 Aqu | 28 Pis | 29 Tau | 28 Gem | 29 Leo | 30 Lib | 30 Sco | 29 Sag | 28 Cap |
|  |  | 30 Cap |  | 30 Ari |  | 30 Can | 31 Vir |  |  |  | 31 Aqu |

### BORN IN THE YEAR 1998

| JAN | FEB | MAR | APR | MAY | JUN | JUL | AUG | SEP | OCT | NOV | DEC |
|-----|-----|-----|-----|-----|-----|-----|-----|-----|-----|-----|-----|
| 2 Pis | 2 Tau | 2 Tau | 2 Can | 2 Leo | 3 Lib | 3 Sco | 2 Sag | 3 Aqu | 2 Pis | 1 Ari | 2 Gem |
| 4 Ari | 4 Gem | 4 Gem | 4 Leo | 4 Vir | 5 Sco | 5 Sag | 4 Cap | 5 Pis | 4 Ari | 3 Tau | 4 Can |
| 6 Tau | 7 Can | 6 Can | 7 Vir | 7 Lib | 8 Sag | 8 Cap | 6 Aqu | 7 Ari | 6 Tau | 5 Gem | 6 Leo |
| 8 Gem | 9 Leo | 8 Leo | 9 Lib | 9 Sco | 10 Cap | 10 Aqu | 8 Pis | 9 Tau | 8 Gem | 7 Can | 9 Vir |
| 10 Can | 11 Vir | 11 Vir | 12 Sco | 12 Sag | 13 Aqu | 12 Pis | 11 Ari | 11 Gem | 10 Can | 9 Leo | 11 Lib |
| 13 Leo | 14 Lib | 13 Lib | 14 Sag | 14 Cap | 15 Pis | 14 Ari | 13 Tau | 13 Can | 13 Leo | 11 Vir | 14 Sco |
| 15 Vir | 16 Sco | 16 Sco | 17 Cap | 16 Aqu | 17 Ari | 16 Tau | 15 Gem | 15 Leo | 15 Vir | 14 Lib | 16 Sag |
| 18 Lib | 19 Sag | 18 Sag | 19 Aqu | 19 Pis | 19 Tau | 18 Gem | 17 Can | 18 Vir | 17 Lib | 16 Sco | 19 Cap |
| 20 Sco | 21 Cap | 21 Cap | 21 Pis | 21 Ari | 21 Gem | 21 Can | 19 Leo | 20 Lib | 20 Sco | 19 Sag | 21 Aqu |
| 23 Sag | 23 Aqu | 23 Aqu | 23 Ari | 23 Tau | 23 Can | 23 Leo | 21 Vir | 23 Sco | 23 Sag | 21 Cap | 23 Pis |
| 25 Cap | 25 Pis | 25 Pis | 25 Tau | 25 Gem | 25 Leo | 25 Vir | 24 Lib | 25 Sag | 25 Cap | 24 Aqu | 25 Ari |
| 27 Aqu | 27 Ari | 27 Ari | 27 Gem | 27 Can | 28 Vir | 28 Lib | 26 Sco | 28 Cap | 27 Aqu | 26 Pis | 28 Tau |
| 29 Pis |  | 29 Tau | 29 Can | 29 Leo | 30 Lib | 30 Sco | 29 Sag | 30 Aqu | 30 Pis | 28 Ari | 30 Gem |
| 31 Ari |  | 31 Gem |  | 31 Vir |  |  | 31 Cap |  |  | 30 Tau |  |

| | JAN | FEB | MAR | APR | MAY | JUN | JUL | AUG | SEP | OCT | NOV | DEC |
|---|---|---|---|---|---|---|---|---|---|---|---|---|

## BORN IN THE YEAR 1999

| JAN | FEB | MAR | APR | MAY | JUN | JUL | AUG | SEP | OCT | NOV | DEC |
|---|---|---|---|---|---|---|---|---|---|---|---|
| 1 Can | 1 Vir | 1 Vir | 2 Sco | 2 Sag | 3 Aqu | 2 Pis | 1 Ari | 2 Gem | 1 Can | 1 Vir | 1 Lib |
| 3 Leo | 4 Lib | 3 Lib | 4 Sag | 4 Cap | 5 Pis | 5 Ari | 3 Tau | 4 Can | 3 Leo | 4 Lib | 3 Sco |
| 5 Vir | 6 Sco | 6 Sco | 7 Cap | 7 Aqu | 8 Ari | 7 Tau | 5 Gem | 6 Leo | 5 Vir | 6 Sco | 6 Sag |
| 7 Lib | 9 Sag | 8 Sag | 9 Aqu | 9 Pis | 10 Tau | 9 Gem | 7 Can | 8 Vir | 8 Lib | 9 Sag | 8 Cap |
| 10 Sco | 11 Cap | 11 Cap | 12 Pis | 11 Ari | 12 Gem | 11 Can | 9 Leo | 10 Lib | 10 Sco | 11 Cap | 11 Aqu |
| 12 Sag | 14 Aqu | 13 Aqu | 14 Ari | 13 Tau | 14 Can | 13 Leo | 12 Vir | 13 Sco | 12 Sag | 14 Aqu | 13 Pis |
| 15 Cap | 16 Pis | 15 Pis | 16 Tau | 15 Gem | 16 Leo | 15 Vir | 14 Lib | 15 Sag | 15 Cap | 16 Pis | 16 Ari |
| 17 Aqu | 18 Ari | 17 Ari | 18 Gem | 17 Can | 18 Vir | 17 Lib | 16 Sco | 18 Cap | 17 Aqu | 18 Ari | 18 Tau |
| 19 Pis | 20 Tau | 19 Tau | 20 Can | 19 Leo | 20 Lib | 20 Sco | 19 Sag | 20 Aqu | 20 Pis | 21 Tau | 20 Gem |
| 22 Ari | 22 Gem | 21 Gem | 22 Leo | 21 Vir | 23 Sco | 22 Sag | 21 Cap | 22 Pis | 22 Ari | 23 Gem | 22 Can |
| 24 Tau | 24 Can | 23 Can | 24 Vir | 24 Lib | 25 Sag | 25 Cap | 24 Aqu | 25 Ari | 24 Tau | 25 Can | 24 Leo |
| 26 Gem | 26 Leo | 26 Leo | 27 Lib | 26 Sco | 28 Cap | 27 Aqu | 26 Pis | 27 Tau | 26 Gem | 27 Leo | 26 Vir |
| 28 Can | | 28 Vir | 29 Sco | 29 Sag | 30 Aqu | 30 Pis | 28 Ari | 29 Gem | 28 Can | 29 Vir | 28 Lib |
| 30 Leo | | 30 Lib | | 31 Cap | | | 30 Tau | | 30 Leo | | 31 Sco |

## BORN IN THE YEAR 2000

| JAN | FEB | MAR | APR | MAY | JUN | JUL | AUG | SEP | OCT | NOV | DEC |
|---|---|---|---|---|---|---|---|---|---|---|---|
| 3 Sag | 1 Cap | 2 Aqu | 1 Pis | 3 Tau | 1 Gem | 2 Leo | 1 Vir | 2 Sco | 1 Sag | 3 Aqu | 2 Pis |
| 5 Cap | 4 Aqu | 4 Pis | 3 Ari | 5 Gem | 3 Can | 4 Vir | 3 Lib | 4 Sag | 4 Cap | 5 Pis | 5 Ari |
| 7 Aqu | 6 Pis | 7 Ari | 5 Tau | 7 Can | 5 Leo | 7 Lib | 5 Sco | 6 Cap | 6 Aqu | 8 Ari | 7 Tau |
| 10 Pis | 8 Ari | 9 Tau | 7 Gem | 9 Leo | 7 Vir | 9 Sco | 8 Sag | 9 Aqu | 9 Pis | 10 Tau | 9 Gem |
| 12 Ari | 11 Tau | 11 Gem | 9 Can | 11 Vir | 9 Lib | 11 Sag | 10 Cap | 11 Pis | 11 Ari | 12 Gem | 11 Can |
| 14 Tau | 13 Gem | 13 Can | 11 Leo | 13 Lib | 12 Sco | 14 Cap | 13 Aqu | 14 Ari | 13 Tau | 14 Can | 13 Leo |
| 16 Gem | 15 Can | 15 Leo | 14 Vir | 15 Sco | 14 Sag | 16 Aqu | 15 Pis | 16 Tau | 16 Gem | 16 Leo | 15 Vir |
| 18 Can | 17 Leo | 17 Vir | 16 Lib | 18 Sag | 17 Cap | 19 Pis | 18 Ari | 18 Gem | 18 Can | 18 Vir | 18 Lib |
| 20 Leo | 19 Vir | 20 Lib | 18 Sco | 20 Cap | 19 Aqu | 21 Ari | 20 Tau | 20 Can | 20 Leo | 20 Lib | 20 Sco |
| 23 Vir | 21 Lib | 22 Sco | 21 Sag | 23 Aqu | 22 Pis | 24 Tau | 22 Gem | 23 Leo | 22 Vir | 23 Sco | 22 Sag |
| 25 Lib | 23 Sco | 24 Sag | 23 Cap | 25 Pis | 24 Ari | 26 Gem | 24 Can | 25 Vir | 24 Lib | 25 Sag | 25 Cap |
| 27 Sco | 26 Sag | 27 Cap | 26 Aqu | 28 Ari | 26 Tau | 28 Can | 26 Leo | 27 Lib | 26 Sco | 27 Cap | 27 Aqu |
| 29 Sag | 28 Cap | 29 Aqu | 28 Pis | 30 Tau | 28 Gem | 30 Leo | 28 Vir | 29 Sco | 29 Sag | 30 Aqu | 30 Pis |
| | | | 30 Ari | | 30 Can | | 30 Lib | | 31 Cap | | |

## BORN IN THE YEAR 2001

| JAN | FEB | MAR | APR | MAY | JUN | JUL | AUG | SEP | OCT | NOV | DEC |
|---|---|---|---|---|---|---|---|---|---|---|---|
| 1 Ari | 2 Gem | 1 Gem | 2 Leo | 1 Vir | 2 Sco | 1 Sag | 3 Aqu | 1 Pis | 1 Ari | 2 Gem | 2 Can |
| 4 Tau | 4 Can | 4 Can | 4 Vir | 3 Lib | 4 Sag | 4 Cap | 5 Pis | 4 Ari | 4 Tau | 4 Can | 4 Leo |
| 6 Gem | 6 Leo | 6 Leo | 6 Lib | 5 Sco | 7 Cap | 6 Aqu | 8 Ari | 6 Tau | 6 Gem | 7 Leo | 6 Vir |
| 8 Can | 8 Vir | 8 Vir | 8 Sco | 8 Sag | 9 Aqu | 9 Pis | 10 Tau | 9 Gem | 8 Can | 9 Vir | 8 Lib |
| 10 Leo | 10 Lib | 10 Lib | 10 Sag | 10 Cap | 11 Pis | 11 Ari | 12 Gem | 11 Can | 10 Leo | 11 Lib | 10 Sco |
| 12 Vir | 12 Sco | 12 Sco | 13 Cap | 13 Aqu | 14 Ari | 14 Tau | 15 Can | 13 Leo | 13 Vir | 13 Sco | 12 Sag |
| 14 Lib | 15 Sag | 14 Sag | 15 Aqu | 15 Pis | 16 Tau | 16 Gem | 17 Leo | 15 Vir | 15 Lib | 15 Sag | 14 Cap |
| 16 Sco | 17 Cap | 16 Cap | 18 Pis | 18 Ari | 19 Gem | 18 Can | 19 Vir | 17 Lib | 17 Sco | 17 Cap | 17 Aqu |
| 18 Sag | 20 Aqu | 19 Aqu | 20 Ari | 20 Tau | 21 Can | 20 Leo | 21 Lib | 19 Sco | 19 Sag | 20 Aqu | 20 Pis |
| 21 Cap | 22 Pis | 22 Pis | 23 Tau | 22 Gem | 23 Leo | 22 Vir | 23 Sco | 21 Sag | 21 Cap | 22 Pis | 22 Ari |
| 23 Aqu | 25 Ari | 24 Ari | 25 Gem | 24 Can | 25 Vir | 24 Lib | 25 Sag | 24 Cap | 23 Aqu | 25 Ari | 25 Tau |
| 26 Pis | 27 Tau | 26 Tau | 27 Can | 27 Leo | 27 Lib | 26 Sco | 27 Cap | 26 Aqu | 26 Pis | 27 Tau | 27 Gem |
| 28 Ari | | 29 Gem | 29 Leo | 29 Vir | 29 Sco | 29 Sag | 30 Aqu | 29 Pis | 28 Ari | 30 Gem | 29 Can |
| 31 Tau | | 31 Can | | 31 Lib | | 31 Cap | | | 31 Tau | | 31 Leo |

## BORN IN THE YEAR 2002

| JAN | FEB | MAR | APR | MAY | JUN | JUL | AUG | SEP | OCT | NOV | DEC |
|---|---|---|---|---|---|---|---|---|---|---|---|
| 2 Vir | 1 Lib | 2 Sco | 1 Sag | 2 Aqu | 1 Pis | 1 Ari | 2 Gem | 1 Can | 1 Leo | 1 Lib | 1 Sco |
| 4 Lib | 3 Sco | 4 Sag | 3 Cap | 5 Pis | 4 Ari | 4 Tau | 5 Can | 3 Leo | 3 Vir | 3 Sco | 3 Sag |
| 6 Sco | 5 Sag | 6 Cap | 5 Aqu | 7 Ari | 6 Tau | 6 Gem | 7 Leo | 5 Vir | 5 Lib | 5 Sag | 5 Cap |
| 9 Sag | 7 Cap | 9 Aqu | 8 Pis | 10 Tau | 9 Gem | 8 Can | 9 Vir | 7 Lib | 7 Sco | 7 Cap | 7 Aqu |
| 11 Cap | 10 Aqu | 11 Pis | 10 Ari | 12 Gem | 11 Can | 11 Leo | 11 Lib | 9 Sco | 9 Sag | 10 Aqu | 9 Pis |
| 13 Aqu | 12 Pis | 14 Ari | 12 Tau | 15 Can | 13 Leo | 13 Vir | 13 Sco | 11 Sag | 12 Cap | 12 Pis | 12 Ari |
| 16 Pis | 15 Ari | 16 Tau | 15 Gem | 17 Leo | 15 Vir | 15 Lib | 15 Sag | 14 Cap | 14 Aqu | 15 Ari | 14 Tau |
| 18 Ari | 17 Tau | 19 Gem | 18 Can | 19 Vir | 18 Lib | 17 Sco | 18 Cap | 16 Aqu | 16 Pis | 17 Tau | 17 Gem |
| 21 Tau | 20 Gem | 21 Can | 20 Leo | 21 Lib | 20 Sco | 19 Sag | 20 Aqu | 19 Pis | 18 Ari | 20 Gem | 19 Can |
| 23 Gem | 22 Can | 24 Leo | 22 Vir | 23 Sco | 22 Sag | 21 Cap | 22 Pis | 21 Ari | 21 Tau | 22 Can | 21 Leo |
| 26 Can | 24 Leo | 26 Vir | 24 Lib | 25 Sag | 24 Cap | 24 Aqu | 25 Ari | 24 Tau | 23 Gem | 24 Leo | 24 Vir |
| 28 Leo | 26 Vir | 28 Lib | 26 Sco | 28 Cap | 26 Aqu | 26 Pis | 27 Tau | 26 Gem | 26 Can | 27 Vir | 26 Lib |
| 30 Vir | 28 Lib | 30 Sco | 28 Sag | 30 Aqu | 29 Pis | 28 Ari | 30 Gem | 29 Can | 28 Leo | 29 Lib | 28 Sco |
| | | | 30 Cap | | | 31 Tau | | | 30 Vir | | 30 Sag |

## BORN IN THE YEAR 2003

| JAN | FEB | MAR | APR | MAY | JUN | JUL | AUG | SEP | OCT | NOV | DEC |
|---|---|---|---|---|---|---|---|---|---|---|---|
| 1 Cap | 2 Pis | 1 Pis | 3 Tau | 2 Gem | 1 Can | 1 Leo | 2 Lib | 2 Sag | 1 Cap | 2 Pis | 2 Ari |
| 3 Aqu | 5 Ari | 4 Ari | 5 Gem | 5 Can | 4 Leo | 3 Vir | 4 Sco | 4 Cap | 4 Aqu | 5 Ari | 4 Tau |
| 6 Pis | 7 Tau | 6 Tau | 8 Can | 7 Leo | 6 Vir | 5 Lib | 6 Sag | 6 Aqu | 6 Pis | 7 Tau | 7 Gem |
| 8 Ari | 10 Gem | 9 Gem | 10 Leo | 10 Vir | 8 Lib | 7 Sco | 8 Cap | 9 Pis | 8 Ari | 10 Gem | 9 Can |
| 11 Tau | 12 Can | 11 Can | 12 Vir | 12 Lib | 10 Sco | 10 Sag | 10 Aqu | 11 Ari | 11 Tau | 12 Can | 12 Leo |
| 13 Gem | 14 Leo | 14 Leo | 14 Lib | 14 Sco | 12 Sag | 12 Cap | 12 Pis | 13 Tau | 13 Gem | 14 Leo | 14 Vir |
| 16 Can | 16 Vir | 16 Vir | 16 Sco | 16 Sag | 14 Cap | 14 Aqu | 15 Ari | 16 Gem | 16 Can | 17 Vir | 16 Lib |
| 18 Leo | 18 Lib | 18 Lib | 18 Sag | 18 Cap | 16 Aqu | 16 Pis | 17 Tau | 18 Can | 18 Leo | 19 Lib | 19 Sco |
| 20 Vir | 21 Sco | 20 Sco | 20 Cap | 20 Aqu | 19 Pis | 18 Ari | 20 Gem | 21 Leo | 21 Vir | 21 Sco | 21 Sag |
| 22 Lib | 23 Sag | 22 Sag | 23 Aqu | 22 Pis | 21 Ari | 21 Tau | 22 Can | 23 Vir | 23 Lib | 23 Sag | 23 Cap |
| 24 Sco | 25 Cap | 24 Cap | 25 Pis | 25 Ari | 23 Tau | 23 Gem | 24 Leo | 25 Lib | 25 Sco | 25 Cap | 25 Aqu |
| 26 Sag | 27 Aqu | 26 Aqu | 27 Ari | 27 Tau | 26 Gem | 26 Can | 27 Vir | 27 Sco | 27 Sag | 27 Aqu | 27 Pis |
| 29 Cap | | 29 Pis | 30 Tau | 30 Gem | 28 Can | 28 Leo | 29 Lib | 29 Sag | 29 Cap | 29 Pis | 29 Ari |
| 31 Aqu | | 31 Ari | | | | 30 Vir | 31 Sco | | 31 Aqu | | |

## BORN IN THE YEAR 2004

| JAN | FEB | MAR | APR | MAY | JUN | JUL | AUG | SEP | OCT | NOV | DEC |
|---|---|---|---|---|---|---|---|---|---|---|---|
| 1 Tau | 2 Can | 3 Leo | 1 Vir | 1 Lib | 2 Sag | 1 Cap | 1 Pis | 2 Tau | 2 Gem | 1 Can | 1 Leo |
| 3 Gem | 4 Leo | 5 Vir | 4 Lib | 3 Sco | 4 Cap | 3 Aqu | 4 Ari | 5 Gem | 5 Can | 3 Leo | 3 Vir |
| 6 Can | 7 Vir | 7 Lib | 6 Sco | 5 Sag | 6 Aqu | 5 Pis | 6 Tau | 7 Can | 7 Leo | 6 Vir | 6 Lib |
| 8 Leo | 9 Lib | 9 Sco | 9 Sag | 7 Cap | 8 Pis | 7 Ari | 8 Gem | 10 Leo | 10 Vir | 8 Lib | 8 Sco |
| 10 Vir | 11 Sco | 12 Sag | 10 Cap | 9 Aqu | 10 Ari | 9 Tau | 11 Can | 12 Vir | 12 Lib | 10 Sco | 10 Sag |
| 13 Lib | 13 Sag | 14 Cap | 12 Aqu | 11 Pis | 12 Tau | 12 Gem | 13 Leo | 14 Lib | 14 Sco | 13 Sag | 12 Cap |
| 15 Sco | 15 Cap | 16 Aqu | 14 Pis | 14 Ari | 15 Gem | 15 Can | 16 Vir | 17 Sco | 16 Sag | 15 Cap | 14 Aqu |
| 17 Sag | 17 Aqu | 18 Pis | 16 Ari | 16 Tau | 17 Can | 17 Leo | 18 Lib | 19 Sag | 18 Cap | 17 Aqu | 16 Pis |
| 19 Cap | 19 Pis | 20 Ari | 18 Tau | 19 Gem | 20 Leo | 20 Vir | 20 Sco | 21 Cap | 20 Aqu | 19 Pis | 18 Ari |
| 21 Aqu | 22 Ari | 23 Tau | 21 Gem | 21 Can | 22 Vir | 22 Lib | 23 Sag | 23 Aqu | 23 Pis | 21 Ari | 21 Tau |
| 23 Pis | 24 Tau | 25 Gem | 24 Can | 24 Leo | 25 Lib | 24 Sco | 25 Cap | 25 Pis | 25 Ari | 23 Tau | 23 Gem |
| 25 Ari | 27 Gem | 28 Can | 26 Leo | 26 Vir | 27 Sco | 26 Sag | 27 Aqu | 27 Ari | 27 Tau | 26 Gem | 25 Can |
| 28 Tau | 29 Can | 30 Leo | 29 Vir | 28 Lib | 29 Sag | 28 Cap | 29 Pis | 30 Tau | 29 Gem | 28 Can | 28 Leo |
| 30 Gem | | | | 31 Sco | | 30 Aqu | 31 Ari | | | | 31 Vir |

## BORN IN THE YEAR 2005

| JAN | FEB | MAR | APR | MAY | JUN | JUL | AUG | SEP | OCT | NOV | DEC |
|---|---|---|---|---|---|---|---|---|---|---|---|
| 2 Lib | 1 Sco | 2 Sag | 3 Aqu | 2 Pis | 3 Tau | 2 Gem | 1 Can | 2 Vir | 2 Lib | 1 Sco | 2 Cap |
| 4 Sco | 3 Sag | 4 Cap | 5 Pis | 4 Ari | 5 Gem | 5 Can | 3 Leo | 5 Lib | 4 Sco | 3 Sag | 4 Aqu |
| 6 Sag | 5 Cap | 6 Aqu | 7 Ari | 6 Tau | 7 Can | 7 Leo | 6 Vir | 7 Sco | 7 Sag | 5 Cap | 7 Pis |
| 8 Cap | 7 Aqu | 8 Pis | 9 Tau | 9 Gem | 10 Leo | 10 Vir | 8 Lib | 9 Sag | 9 Cap | 7 Aqu | 9 Ari |
| 10 Aqu | 9 Pis | 10 Ari | 11 Gem | 11 Can | 12 Vir | 12 Lib | 11 Sco | 12 Cap | 11 Aqu | 9 Pis | 11 Tau |
| 12 Pis | 11 Ari | 13 Tau | 14 Can | 14 Leo | 15 Lib | 15 Sco | 13 Sag | 14 Aqu | 13 Pis | 11 Ari | 13 Gem |
| 15 Ari | 13 Tau | 15 Gem | 16 Leo | 16 Vir | 17 Sco | 17 Sag | 15 Cap | 16 Pis | 15 Ari | 14 Tau | 15 Can |
| 17 Tau | 16 Gem | 17 Can | 18 Vir | 18 Lib | 19 Sag | 19 Cap | 17 Aqu | 18 Ari | 17 Tau | 16 Gem | 18 Leo |
| 19 Gem | 18 Can | 20 Leo | 21 Lib | 21 Sco | 21 Cap | 21 Aqu | 19 Pis | 20 Tau | 19 Gem | 18 Can | 20 Vir |
| 22 Can | 21 Leo | 22 Vir | 23 Sco | 23 Sag | 23 Aqu | 23 Pis | 21 Ari | 22 Gem | 22 Can | 21 Leo | 23 Lib |
| 24 Leo | 23 Vir | 25 Lib | 26 Sag | 25 Cap | 25 Pis | 25 Ari | 23 Tau | 24 Can | 24 Leo | 23 Vir | 25 Sco |
| 27 Vir | 25 Lib | 27 Sco | 28 Cap | 27 Aqu | 28 Ari | 27 Tau | 26 Gem | 27 Leo | 27 Vir | 26 Lib | 28 Sag |
| 29 Lib | 28 Sco | 29 Sag | 30 Aqu | 29 Pis | 30 Tau | 29 Gem | 28 Can | 29 Vir | 29 Lib | 28 Sco | 30 Cap |
| | | 31 Cap | | 31 Ari | | | 31 Leo | | | 30 Sag | |

## BORN IN THE YEAR 2006

| JAN | FEB | MAR | APR | MAY | JUN | JUL | AUG | SEP | OCT | NOV | DEC |
|---|---|---|---|---|---|---|---|---|---|---|---|
| 1 Aqu | 1 Ari | 1 Ari | 1 Gem | 1 Can | 2 Vir | 2 Lib | 1 Sco | 2 Cap | 1 Aqu | 2 Ari | 1 Tau |
| 3 Pis | 3 Tau | 3 Tau | 4 Can | 3 Leo | 5 Lib | 5 Sco | 3 Sag | 4 Aqu | 4 Pis | 4 Tau | 3 Gem |
| 5 Ari | 6 Gem | 5 Gem | 6 Leo | 6 Vir | 7 Sco | 7 Sag | 6 Cap | 6 Pis | 6 Ari | 6 Gem | 6 Can |
| 7 Tau | 8 Can | 7 Can | 9 Vir | 8 Lib | 10 Sag | 9 Cap | 8 Aqu | 8 Ari | 8 Tau | 8 Can | 8 Leo |
| 9 Gem | 10 Leo | 10 Leo | 11 Lib | 11 Sco | 12 Cap | 11 Aqu | 10 Pis | 10 Tau | 10 Gem | 10 Leo | 10 Vir |
| 12 Can | 13 Vir | 12 Vir | 13 Sco | 13 Sag | 14 Aqu | 13 Pis | 12 Ari | 12 Gem | 12 Can | 13 Vir | 13 Lib |
| 14 Leo | 16 Lib | 15 Lib | 16 Sag | 15 Cap | 16 Pis | 15 Ari | 14 Tau | 14 Can | 14 Leo | 15 Lib | 15 Sco |
| 17 Vir | 18 Sco | 17 Sco | 18 Cap | 18 Aqu | 18 Ari | 17 Tau | 16 Gem | 17 Leo | 17 Vir | 18 Sco | 18 Sag |
| 19 Lib | 20 Sag | 20 Sag | 20 Aqu | 20 Pis | 20 Tau | 20 Gem | 18 Can | 19 Vir | 19 Lib | 20 Sag | 20 Cap |
| 22 Sco | 23 Cap | 22 Cap | 22 Pis | 22 Ari | 22 Gem | 22 Can | 21 Leo | 22 Lib | 22 Sco | 23 Cap | 22 Aqu |
| 24 Sag | 25 Aqu | 24 Aqu | 25 Ari | 24 Tau | 25 Can | 24 Leo | 23 Vir | 24 Sco | 24 Sag | 25 Aqu | 24 Pis |
| 26 Cap | 27 Pis | 26 Pis | 27 Tau | 26 Gem | 27 Leo | 27 Vir | 26 Lib | 27 Sag | 26 Cap | 27 Pis | 27 Ari |
| 28 Aqu | | 28 Ari | 29 Gem | 28 Can | 29 Vir | 29 Lib | 28 Sco | 29 Cap | 29 Aqu | 29 Ari | 29 Tau |
| 30 Pis | | 30 Tau | | 31 Leo | | | 31 Sag | | 31 Pis | | 31 Gem |

# WHAT YOUR MOON SIGN SAYS ABOUT YOU

*Now that you know your Moon sign, read on to learn more about your emotional nature and your basic inner needs.*

### MOON IN ARIES

You have an emotional need to be first. And you want to be first *now*—there's no time to waste. Brimming with enthusiasm and energy, you love to keep busy and find waiting difficult. Remember to open up and talk to those closest to you about your feelings—they can help you to slow down and deal with any difficult emotions as they arise.

### MOON IN TAURUS

You love to be surrounded by beautiful possessions and enjoy food and clothes that make you feel good—you have a need for comfort. Familiarity and routine are important to you, and you don't deal well with sudden change. That stubborn streak means you're able to stand up for yourself and protect your own interests, Just remember to relax once in a while and try new things.

### MOON IN GEMINI

Self-expression is one of your driving forces with this mix. Talking, drawing, writing—you simply have to communicate your feelings. And you love to listen to other peoples' ideas, too. To feed your curious intellect, you've probably got a tower of books and magazines at your bedside. Just don't forget to exercise your body as well as your mind.

### MOON IN CANCER

You were born to nurture others—whether that's through baking them a cake or being at the end of the phone when they need your reassuring words. Family is hugely important to you, and you want to feel loved and secure. Being honest about this and accepting your wonderfully sensitive and emotional nature will help you find inner peace.

### MOON IN LEO

You have an emotional need to be admired—all you really want is for everyone to love you. Your kind heart and generosity toward your friends and family means you are usually surrounded by others, and the attention you crave is easily won. When things don't go your way, you have a tendency to be dramatic—don't let your pride stop you from asking for help when you need it.

### MOON IN VIRGO

You are a gentle soul and appreciate the simple things in life. Helping others in small ways makes you feel needed, secure, and purposeful. A clean and tidy environment is a must, and everything has to be in its proper place. Learning not to fuss when something isn't perfect is a challenge—look for useful ways to keep your practical nature busy and happiness will follow.

### MOON IN LIBRA

Close bonds are everything to you—you find strength and stability in your relationships with others. Your need for balance and harmony means you are an excellent peacemaker, skilled at helping people to see and understand another's perspective. Remember to feed your love of beauty with regular trips to art galleries and picturesque places.

### MOON IN SCORPIO

Deep and emotionally intense, you need to trust those close to you with your innermost thoughts and desires. All or nothing, you have incredible intuition and can see right to the heart of people. Finding one or two close friends who you can really open up to and be honest with about your feelings is important for your happiness. When this happens, your inner strength is unmatched.

### MOON IN SAGITTARIUS

Your need for freedom and space is overwhelming, but when you achieve it, you are bright, breezy, and filled with a zest for life. Always on the lookout for new things to try and people to meet, your energy and enthusiasm lifts the spirits of those around you. Planning is not your strong suit; you prefer to go with the flow and see where it takes you—preferably somewhere fun and interesting!

### MOON IN CAPRICORN

Ambitious and practical, you want to work hard and achieve results. You are conscientious and naturally organized, with a clear picture of what you want and how you intend to get there. Remember to take time to kick back and relax—the strong front you present to those around you can hide your more sensitive side. Letting go occasionally isn't a sign of weakness.

### MOON IN AQUARIUS

Your desire to be unique and unusual is powerful, and you need the space and freedom to be yourself. Emotionally detached, you are happily independent and have an ability to see the bigger picture. Try not to lose touch with those closest to you—life is full of ups and downs, and friends and family can offer valuable support through tougher times.

### MOON IN PISCES

Dreamy and intuitive, your sensitive nature is highly attuned to the feelings of others. Be careful to steer clear of negative people—you're likely to absorb their vibes, and they will bring you down. It's important you learn how to take care of yourself when you feel overwhelmed emotionally. Escaping into a good book or listening to your favorite music can be a great way to reset.

ELEMENTS

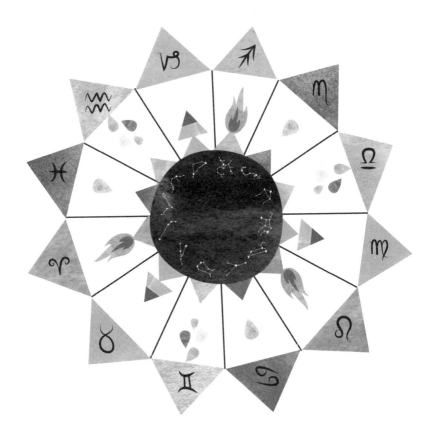

# YOUR ELEMENTAL TYPE

Fire, Earth, Air, Water—in ancient times these were thought to contain everything that existed on Earth. Today that's no longer the case, but there's no denying their powerful effect on people's lives. Think of the heat from the Sun, the way earth is used to grow food, the water you consume, the air that you breathe. And like so much in astrology, each element has two sides. You drink water and rain helps plants to grow, but the force of a tsunami can wreak havoc and destruction. You have all four elements within you, but one or more of them will stand out. You could be a single type, or a mix of two or three. Your elemental type says a lot about you and those you interact with. When you meet someone you feel naturally comfortable with, it's often because you are elementally compatible.

# IN YOUR ELEMENT

A typical Fire sign, Sagittarius is lively and playful. You're out to have a good time, and you don't mind if you overdo things a little along the way. Adventurous and optimistic, you find routine stifling and are ready to experience everything life has to offer. At your best you are radiant and bring light to the world around you; at your worst your burning idealism can blind you to others' points of view.

 FIRE WITH FIRE

You get along well with other Fire signs, just as Earth will with Earth, and so on. Relationships are led by the heart rather than by the head, as you both love others freely and with your whole being. When arguments arise, sparks can fly. Cool off with a walk or some kind of physical activity.

 FIRE WITH EARTH

Not ideally compatible, as Earth extinguishes fire, while "scorched Earth" is sterile and unproductive. Still, Earth can slow you down, acting as a grounding force, while you might get them going, energizing them with your passion and intensity. Finding a balance between stability and some form of newness and excitement is essential to a happy relationship.

 FIRE WITH AIR

Fire and Air signs are wonderfully compatible—think of oxygen to a flame. Air is full of ideas, and you are ready to put them into action. Together, you are a powerful, unstoppable force of activity. Remember, though, that relationships can become overwhelming if boundaries aren't put in place—Air has the ability to fuel Fire, but it can also blow it out.

 FIRE WITH WATER

Not an ideal mix. Fire and Water can be beautiful together, adventurous and dynamic, but if one is too dominant, it can dampen Fire's energy or scorch Water's emotions. When it works, Water will bring sensitivity and comfort, while you provide motivation and the courage to act.

# THE MISSING PIECE

How dominant Fire is within you depends on the influence of the other elements in your chart—ideally all four would be represented. Sometimes a lack of a particular element can cause an imbalance, making you feel rundown or stressed. The best way to counteract this is to tune in to the missing element and reharmonize yourself. Try the simple exercise below to get back in touch with any elements you're missing.

1. First, take a look at the Zodiac signs and their elements.

**Fire:** Aries, Leo, Sagittarius

**Earth:** Taurus, Virgo, Capricorn

**Air:** Gemini, Libra, Aquarius

**Water:** Cancer, Scorpio, Pisces

2. Now circle Fire, as this is the element that represents your Sun sign. You're certain to have some of this element. Then do the same for your Moon sign and your Ascendant, circling the element associated with each.

3. Looking at the list, there should be one or more elements you haven't circled.

**Earth**—a lack of Earth can make you feel disorganized, off-balance, or like you couldn't care less. You might want more routine, structure, or to stay focused.

**Air**—Air will help you to communicate better, feel more sociable, and lift your spirits. Use it to boost your curiosity and sharpen your wits.

**Water**—with Water missing you may struggle to get in touch with your emotions or worry you're being insensitive. You're looking to express yourself, to feel more creative and inspired.

4. Choose the element you would like to tune in to, whichever one you feel might benefit you. Then pick one of the ideas from the lists below. If Earth is missing, you could take a picnic to the park and sit on the grass. If it's Water, you could try a soak in the tub. You can use this exercise whenever you feel out of balance.

### EARTH

Grow tomatoes
Pick wildflowers
Collect stones
Camp in the garden
Do cartwheels on the grass
Build a sandcastle
Roll down a hill

### AIR

Fly a kite
Watch clouds go by
Blow bubbles
Feel the breeze
Breathe deep
Play with a balloon
Chase butterflies

### WATER

Spend a day at the beach
Splash in a puddle
Sit by a fountain
Walk in the rain
Catch a wave
Snorkel

We are
FAMILY

# WE'RE ALL IN THIS TOGETHER

When so much in your life is changing, your relationships with your parents can become even more important. If you're lucky, you get along well with yours, but even the most harmonious relationships can come under strain during the teenage years. How can astrology help? It can remind you that parents are people, too. They might not get everything right, but hopefully you believe that they have your best interests at heart. Learning more about who they are, why they do things, and how you relate to them can make it easier for all of you to move forward together.

## MOTHER MOON

The Moon sign you are born with can tell you a lot about how you see and treat your mother. This is because your Moon sign represents your emotional needs—what you need to feel safe and secure—and these are most often fulfilled by your mother. How you react to her can make a big difference to the way she behaves around you. If you are visibly upset by certain things she does, she is likely to change her behavior the next time around. If you react with happiness and delight, she is more likely to repeat them.

*Here's how you see your mother according to your Moon sign . . .*

## ARIES

You view your mother as strong, honest, and forthright. Sometimes, especially when she doesn't agree with your plans, this can make you feel as though she's taking over. Try not to push back too strongly, and remember she has your interests at heart.

## TAURUS

You like to feel your mother is looking after all of your everyday needs and is dependable and reliable. Don't judge her too harshly if she doesn't always live up to your expectations—providing for others is often a careful balancing act, and she is likely doing her best.

## GEMINI

Flighty and impulsive, you need your mother to give you the freedom to be yourself and make your own mistakes. Space and independence often have to be earned, though—what could you do to show her you're capable and trustworthy?

## CANCER

Your longing for your mother's emotional attention can give you a wonderful bond and connection. However, the slightest hint of rejection from her can wound you deeply. Try not to take her reactions personally—it's okay for her to make choices and have goals that differ from yours.

### LEO

You want to enjoy an open, honest relationship with your mother, where both of you say what you mean. Underlying this candor is a need for assurance and acceptance—when you feel vulnerable, be brave and explain to her how you feel.

### VIRGO

You are aware of who gives what in your emotional relationship with your mother, and occasionally this can make you feel that she isn't there for you. Viewing her actions as "different" rather than "wrong" will help you to trust she is doing what she thinks is right.

### LIBRA

You need your mother to recognize your emotional needs as valid and important. Try not to spend too much time putting others first—your relationship will flourish when you both accept the roles you play.

### SCORPIO

You want your mother to respect your emotional boundaries and allow you alone-time when you need it. The trust between you can be intense and unconditional, so much so you may have to remind her to step back occasionally.

### SAGITTARIUS

Upbeat and curious, your relationship works best when your mother is inspiring and encouraging, giving you the emotional freedom you need to expand your horizons. It's fine to chase independence, as long as you respect your mother's desire to give you roots.

### CAPRICORN

You empathize strongly with your mother's feelings, so when she's struggling, this can make you feel it's your fault. Learn to let go of this guilt—it's unintentional and unhelpful. Instead, recognize how much you need each other's emotional support and encouragement.

### AQUARIUS

You're not sure your mother's attempts to guide you are always necessary, and you don't like to burden her with your problems. Asking for help and talking things through might be more useful than you imagine and can bring you closer together at the same time.

### PISCES

Your mother's high expectations have made you stronger emotionally, even though there are times when you just want to feel like a child and let her take care of everything. Taking responsibility can be tough; don't be afraid to speak up when you need support.

## HOW YOU SEE YOUR FATHER

Just as your Moon sign gives you an indication of how you see your mother, or whoever plays that nurturing role in your life, your Sun sign can reveal the way you view your father, or the caregiver who is most involved with discipline. Your relationship with this person is built over time. For girls, it can have a strong bearing on how you view any future romantic relationships, whereas boys will either rebel or identify with these traits.

If Sagittarius is your Sun sign, you see your father as a great adventurer. He loves to whisk the family away to explore new places, so you never know what's around the corner. And if money is tight, he transports you to another world by reading your favorite book at bedtime.

Now read on to find out how your father's Sun sign affects your relationship . . .

*Your father's Sun sign will play a significant part in how you relate to him, and it can help you to understand why he acts the way he does— however infuriating it may sometimes seem!*

### ARIES

A shared love of make-believe gives you a special bond, and even as you get older, you might still (secretly) love to have your dad read your favorite story to you. Happily, this level of communication is likely to continue throughout your life.

### TAURUS

Sometimes the lines get fraught between the roles in this relationship. Your love of fun can cause your father to worry. If you talk it through, however, they'll hopefully see that you're more responsible than they think.

### GEMINI

You are both "seekers" of the Zodiac, concerned with life's bigger questions and determined to find the answers. Try not to let this disrupt your regular daily routines too much or it'll drive the rest of the family to distraction.

### CANCER

Fun, fun, and more fun is the hallmark of this relationship. You'll create wonderful memories together, going off on exciting adventures or simply laughing at everyday events. Your Sagittarian cheerfulness is a joy for your dad.

### LEO

This is a fine pairing because you complement each other so well. Your playful nature encourages your dad's mischievous side. You probably enjoy setting up elaborate pranks—and see the funny side when you're on the receiving end.

### VIRGO

If anyone is looking for you two, they'll probably find you huddled at the laptop, searching for information. You both soak up knowledge like a sponge and may even consider applying for a TV quiz show, cheering each other on.

### LIBRA

Both of these star signs like to look on the bright side of life and sometimes underplay problems. You rarely give your father cause to be firm with you—just as well, because they hate to do it!

### SCORPIO

There's a lovely learning curve in this special relationship. While you share a sense of urgency about life, your dad can teach you to look before you leap. Equally, your Sagittarius humor can encourage your Scorpio father to take more risks.

### SAGITTARIUS

You are both carefree souls, so it might be tricky to work out who is the parent and who is the child. And you have the power to read each other like a book, meaning there's rarely any secrets between you.

### CAPRICORN

You can sometimes find it hard to connect with each other. Capricorn has a wise, old-soul quality that a firecracker Sagittarius doesn't immediately understand. But don't worry, the relationship is likely to flourish as the years go by.

### AQUARIUS

Equally able to see the bigger picture, the two of you can defuse any tense situation. Usually, you bump along together rather nicely, but if things do take a tricky turn, harmony and mutual respect tend to be quickly restored.

### PISCES

You both seem to always be on the move. That's because you are adaptable signs, able to change in a heartbeat. Your dad cherishes those warm, friendly hugs you more often than not have waiting for him.

Best of
FRIENDS

# FRIENDS FOR LIFE

Friends play an essential role in your happiness. They can help you to move forward when times are tough, see things from a new perspective, and encourage you just to have fun. Every good friend you make has different qualities that will influence you and allow you to make more of your potential. A friend might show you it can be better to hold back when all you want to do is rush in, motivate you to stick with that project right to the end, or inspire you to see an obstacle as a challenge. And astrology can be a great way to highlight those characteristics you're looking for in a friend. It can also tell you more about the type of friend you make for others.

## WHAT KIND OF FRIEND ARE YOU?

Easygoing, positive, and happy-go-lucky, you're a low-maintenance friend. You're up for anything, so you're the first one people will call when they're feeling adventurous. Your friendship circle is wide, as you're open to people from all walks of life. Unguarded and expansive, you manage to connect with strangers almost immediately. Your love of freedom means you refuse to be pinned down.

**Strengths:** *Adventurous, positive, open-minded*
**Weaknesses:** *Impatient, insensitive, easily bored*
**Friendship style:** *Generous, undemanding, never dull*

# IF YOUR BEST FRIEND IS . . .

### ARIES

Aries make friends easily. They're willing to help you achieve your goals, they see the best in you, and they're happy to take risks for you, too. They love to be someone's best friend and can find it difficult to feel second to anyone else. They are always on the lookout for new, super-fun adventures and are happy to take you along for the ride. They have a knack for bringing people from all walks of life together.

**Strengths:** *Loyal, generous, fun-loving*
**Weaknesses:** *Insensitive, demanding, petulant*
**Friendship style:** *Busy, fun, warm*

### TAURUS

Considerate and charming, Taurus friends often have a talent for giving good advice. They like to take their time and allow friendships to develop slowly, but once you become close they treat you as a member of their family. As an Earth sign, they are dependable and grounded, and they make wonderful lifelong friends. Bear in mind they can place too much importance on material possessions, even judging others based on their wealth.

**Strengths:** *Caring, faithful, trustworthy*
**Weaknesses:** *Judgmental, stubborn, materialistic*
**Friendship style:** *Helpful, sweet, self-assured*

### GEMINI

You'll need lots of energy to keep up with a Gemini friend. They love to have fun, do crazy things, and always have a story to tell. They'll make you laugh, but they can sometimes get a little carried away, perhaps exaggerating tales of their adventures in their effort to entertain you. They can be a bit gossipy, but they're not malicious. They're good listeners and will make you feel great, giving you lots of compliments—and always genuine ones, too.

**Strengths:** *Intelligent, energetic, fearless*
**Weaknesses:** *Impatient, easily bored, gossipy*
**Friendship style:** *Good listener, witty, spontaneous*

### CANCER

Once you form a close connection with Cancer, you have a friend who has your back. They're considerate and like nothing better than to make you feel happy. Watch out though; they're deeply emotional, which means that if you argue—even over something small—you'll have to work hard to patch things up again.

**Strengths:** *Loving, caring, intuitive*
**Weaknesses:** *Unforgiving, anxious, sensitive*
**Friendship style:** *Warm, affectionate, protective*

## LEO

As long as you don't expect too much from a Leo friend, you're in for a treat. Outgoing, confident, and full of energy, they thrive on social occasions and love to be the life and soul of a party, making people laugh and being admired. They're good at bringing people together and are in high demand, so you won't always have them to yourself, but if you can tie them down, you'll have some great quality one-on-one time.

**Strengths:** *Honest, brave, positive*
**Weaknesses:** *Arrogant, self-centered, proud*
**Friendship style:** *Supportive, cheerful, humorous*

## VIRGO

With a Virgo by your side you'll always have somewhere to go when times are tough. They'll be there for you, giving you well-thought-out advice and a gentle sympathetic ear. Even when there's not a crisis, they're charming and kind. They like to be organized, so if they make plans, make sure you stick to them. They won't let you down, but they'll expect the same from you in return.

**Strengths:** *Warm, modest, smart*
**Weaknesses:** *Shy, serious, overly critical*
**Friendship style:** *Fixer, good communicator, reliable*

## LIBRA

You can rely on your Libra friend to tell you how it is. They have a refreshing honesty, but they have a diplomatic way of sparing your feelings. They love spending time with you and like nothing better than a chat (especially if they're the one doing the talking!). They can always see both sides, so if there's a disagreement it won't be for long.

**Strengths:** *Diplomatic, honest, sociable*
**Weaknesses:** *Indecisive, people pleaser, chatterbox*
**Friendship style:** *Laid-back, devoted, forgiving*

## SCORPIO

It's an honor to be a Scorpio's best friend. They're selective, so they don't always have many, but the friendships they do make will be really special. Once you've cemented your friendship, they'll open their inner circle to you and will want to spend lots of time together. In return, they'll expect 100 percent loyalty and might not take it well if you let them down, so tread carefully.

**Strengths:** *Passionate, hospitable, perceptive*
**Weaknesses:** *Guarded, jealous, suspicious*
**Friendship style:** *Intense, selective, highly loyal*

### CAPRICORN

You might have to put in some groundwork, but once you've cracked the seemingly aloof exterior of a Capricorn, you'll have yourself a genuine, warm, loving, and faithful friend. They'll show you complete devotion, through the good times and the bad. They're thoughtful and sensible and will know when to call it a night, but they will often surprise you with their sly sense of humor. They love to make you smile.

**Strengths:** *Responsible, supportive, faithful*
**Weaknesses:** *Condescending, standoffish, serious*
**Friendship style:** *Thoughtful, rational, work hard/play hard*

### AQUARIUS

You'll have to share your Aquarius best friend—they'll probably flit in and out of lots of other friendships, too—but rest assured they've got your back and will go to the ends of the earth for you. They'll bring plenty of excitement and fun into your world, but they also treasure their alone time, so don't put too many demands on them. They'll never pass judgment on you, no matter what you do.

**Strengths:** *Tolerant, independent, energetic*
**Weaknesses:** *Easily bored, rebellious, forgetful*
**Friendship style:** *Fun, exciting, unpredictable*

### PISCES

A Pisces friend is a great listener who is sympathetic and caring and will always make time for you. They're the perfect friend if you need a shoulder to cry on, but they can sometimes get too emotionally involved. If there is any discord in your friendship, they are quick to blame themselves. Reassure them and let them know it's not their fault and you'll soon win back their love and support.

**Strengths:** *Loving, caring, good listener*
**Weaknesses:** *Sensitive, self-pitying, insecure*
**Friendship style:** *Supportive, sympathetic, selfless*

# Your BIRTHDAY log

*List the birthdays of your family and friends and discover their Sun signs*

# ARIES

March 21–April 20

*Passionate, energetic, impulsive*

# TAURUS

April 21–May 21

*Steady, tenacious, trustworthy*

# GEMINI
May 22–June 21

*Intelligent, outgoing, witty*

# CANCER

June 22–July 22

*Caring, home-loving, affectionate*

# LEO

July 23–August 23

*Loud, big-hearted, fun*

# VIRGO

August 24–September 22

*Organized, modest, responsible*

# LIBRA

September 23–October 22

*Charming, creative, graceful*

# SCORPIO

October 23–November 21

*Powerful, mysterious, magnetic*

# SAGITTARIUS

November 22–December 21

*Adventurous, optimistic, lucky*

# CAPRICORN

December 22–January 20

*Ambitious, dedicated, serious*

# AQUARIUS

January 21–February 19

*Eccentric, independent, imaginative*

# PISCES

*Dreamy, sensitive, compassionate*

Lucky in
LOVE

# WHY OPPOSITES REALLY DO ATTRACT

The sign opposite your Ascendant (your Rising sign) on your birth chart reveals who you will attract, and who will attract you. Known as your Descendant, it's the constellation that was setting on the Western horizon at the moment and place you were born.

This sign is everything you are not—a kind of mirror image, or two sides of the same coin.

Yet, strangely, you are often drawn to the qualities of this sign over and over again in the people you meet. It's possible that these characteristics are ones you feel you lack yourself, and you sense that the other person can fill in what's missing. Sometimes it really is true that opposites attract!

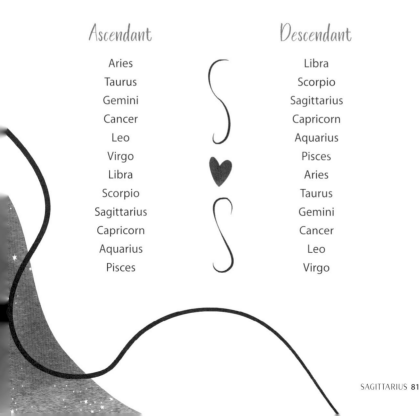

| Ascendant | Descendant |
|---|---|
| Aries | Libra |
| Taurus | Scorpio |
| Gemini | Sagittarius |
| Cancer | Capricorn |
| Leo | Aquarius |
| Virgo | Pisces |
| Libra | Aries |
| Scorpio | Taurus |
| Sagittarius | Gemini |
| Capricorn | Cancer |
| Aquarius | Leo |
| Pisces | Virgo |

# WHAT DO YOU LOOK FOR?

*Once you've matched up your Ascendant with your Descendant from the list on the previous page, you can get to know the qualities that are most likely to attract you. You can use this information whether you're thinking about romance or friendship.*

### LIBRA DESCENDANT

You're looking for balance and harmony in your relationship, with someone who makes you feel interesting and important. You want to be listened to and value the ability to compromise. Gentleness and sensitivity are the qualities you're searching for.

### SCORPIO DESCENDANT

You want an intense, passionate relationship with someone who will welcome you wholeheartedly into their world and want to spend lots of time with you. You are attracted to someone who will take control, but who will also look out for you and protect you.

### SAGITTARIUS DESCENDANT

Adventure and fun are what you crave when it comes to love. You want someone open-minded who will accept you for who you are. You need to be given plenty of space to breathe and not be stifled by too many demands.

### CAPRICORN DESCENDANT

You seek total dedication and devotion from those you love. You're happy to take your time and let a relationship develop naturally, and aren't put off by someone who appears cool or guarded. You like an irreverent sense of humor, too.

### AQUARIUS DESCENDANT

You are attracted to someone who is independent and has a full life outside of your relationship, although you want to know that if push comes to shove, they will be right there for you. You like to be kept on your toes.

### PISCES DESCENDANT

You're not afraid of a deep relationship with someone who wears their heart on their sleeve. You want to be cared for, emotionally supported, and loved unconditionally. You want to be the center of someone's world.

### ARIES DESCENDANT

You like someone to spar with and who lets you have your own way, but is still strong enough to put their foot down when the gravity of the situation demands it. You will need to respect your partner's strength, bravery, and integrity.

### TAURUS DESCENDANT

Stability and reliability are high on your list of priorities when it comes to forming relationships. You dislike chaos and are drawn to people who you know won't surprise or disappoint you. Instead you want a partnership that's grounded and safe.

### GEMINI DESCENDANT

You're attracted to someone who is spontaneous and fearless, and who can keep you entertained. You're likely to fall for someone who makes you feel super-special and is quick to recognize your achievements and boost your confidence.

### CANCER DESCENDANT

You seek relationships where you're made to feel like one of the family, where your every need and demand is met, particularly emotionally. You want to feel warm and fuzzy and protected by those you love.

### LEO DESCENDANT

You're drawn to someone who is strong, confident, and outgoing with a busy social life but who can also give you warmth and passion when required. You're attracted to those who can make you laugh and sweep you off your feet.

### VIRGO DESCENDANT

You long for kindness and tenderness in a partnership, along with reliability. You want someone who can bring order into your life and who will think things through in a methodical way. Nothing should be left to chance.

Life at
SCHOOL

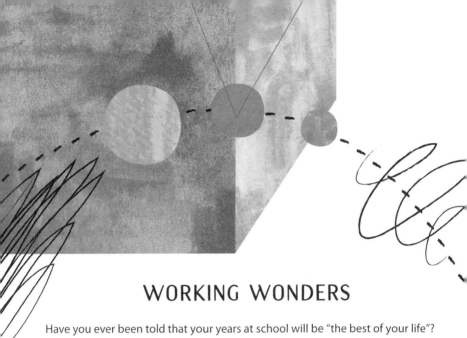

# WORKING WONDERS

Have you ever been told that your years at school will be "the best of your life"? Do you think they will be? Why? Many different things will determine how much you enjoy your school days. And there are sure to be ups and downs along the way. But there are a couple of important factors that astrology can help with. The first is determining your skills and strengths, and the second is learning to work well with others. Identifying your natural interests and abilities can help you to develop a sense of purpose, and it's this that is most likely to motivate you to work hard and actually have fun while you do it. To have a sense of purpose, you need to know yourself and what it is you want from your life. Not what others want for you, or what is expected of you, but what actually makes you come alive.

## HIDDEN TALENTS

Not all of your attributes will be immediately obvious. Just because you're a Sagittarius doesn't necessarily mean you always feel enthusiastic, for example. You can think about what a typical Sagittarius might be good at, but you are unique, and the stars are only a guide. Think about your strengths—both emotional and physical. The examples on the right may strike a chord with you, or you might want to create your own list.

### BECAUSE YOU'RE ... OUTGOING

You are talkative and extroverted, and enjoy group scenarios. You can think on your feet and like to make quick decisions. You usually act first and think later.

*Maybe you could be a ...*
salesperson, hospitality worker, missionary

### BECAUSE YOU'RE ... ENERGETIC

You are a doer more than a thinker and take action to make things happen. Getting things done quickly is more important to you than doing something perfectly. You love to achieve things, have bundles of energy, and work very hard.

*Maybe you could be a ...*
lawyer, taxi driver, sports coach, blogger

### BECAUSE YOU'RE ... CARING

You like to work with other people, especially when their well-being and development is the focus of your work.

*Maybe you could be a ...*
teacher, translator, charity worker

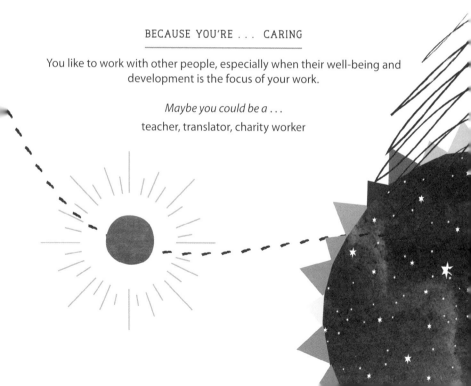

## BECAUSE YOU'RE . . . A LEADER

You love to persuade other people to do something, buy something, or believe in your cause. You're great at influencing and motivating others.

*Maybe you could be a . . .*
fundraiser, explorer, entrepreneur

## BECAUSE YOU'RE . . . AN OVERSEER

You are able to see the bigger picture. You are good at recognizing the important points in lots of information. You look at all the possibilities and narrow these down to the best.

*Maybe you could be a . . .*
manager, travel agent, environmental engineer

# FAMOUS SAGITTARIUS PEOPLE

Scarlett Johansson—*Actor*
Emily Dickinson—*Poet*
Steven Spielberg—*Film director*
Jason Reynolds—*Author*
Brad Pitt—*Actor*
Bruce Lee—*Actor and martial artist*
Taylor Swift—*Pop singer*

# TEAM WORK

*Working together with others is essential for almost any career path you choose to follow in later life. School can be competitive, yet working in collaboration with your peers rather than against them builds skills that today's employers are looking for.*

*Here's how well you work together with . . .*

### ARIES

You both have so much energy and enthusiasm you'll get things done in record time, but try not to rush. It will be easy to get carried away, so make a concerted effort to occasionally stop and make sure you're on the right track, paying closer attention to detail. Pace yourselves, and the results could be wonderful.

### TAURUS

Combine your energy, enthusiasm, and sense of adventure with the bull's dependability, patience, and practicality, and this unlikely pairing could work. As long as they don't take things too seriously and spoil your fun, and as long as you listen to their voice of reason when you're tempted to go off script.

### GEMINI

You're both free spirits with a sense of adventure, so you will easily inspire each other to come up with ideas. Neither of you like routine, but you love a challenge, so motivation won't be an issue. Just make sure you complete one job properly before you move on to the next.

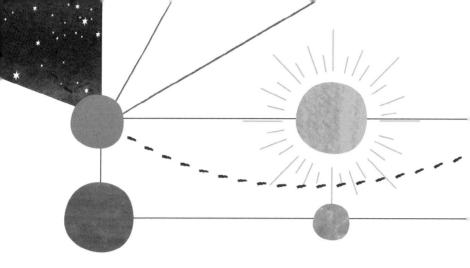

### CANCER

As long as you give each other plenty of room to breathe, this partnership will work well. If not, you'll risk hurting Cancer's feelings, and Cancer risks dampening your adventurous spirit. It's a fine balance but, if achieved, can reap rewards.

### LEO

When you two Fire signs combine your charms, there's no stopping you. You're both blessed with a natural energy and drive, and, when you're members of the same team, you'll feed off each other with remarkable results. You're so well matched, you're hard to beat.

### VIRGO

It's not always smooth sailing when you two come together, but it's not for lack of trying. Virgo's perfectionism works best when it's focused on the minute details, while your time is better spent taking in the bigger picture and painting with a broader brush.

### LIBRA

Whatever you two work on together, it will be a peaceful, harmonious experience from start to finish. You'll work particularly well on more meaningful projects—perhaps for a charity—when you'll both get lots of satisfaction from working for the greater good.

### SCORPIO

You might have completely different ideas about how to get there, but at least you both agree that you want to succeed. To get the best out of this partnership, Scorpio needs to open up a bit, and you might do well to think before you speak. It will pay off in the end.

### SAGITTARIUS

When it comes to brainstorming, you'll have to set strict time limits on meetings as it will be hard to stop once you two get going. Left to your own devices you could end up outside the box, and you won't be able to find your way back in again! Be clear about your objectives and don't get carried away.

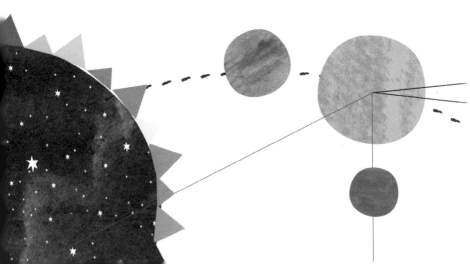

### CAPRICORN

You might struggle to see eye to eye when it comes to how you work. Your approaches are so dissimilar. You'll want to go out and explore an idea in the wider world, while Capricorn prefers to do it the "proper" way, following the correct procedures. Hopefully you'll reach the same conclusion in the end.

### AQUARIUS

The ideas will be flying around the room when you two put your heads together, and they'll all be good, but therein lies your problem. Which ones do you choose? If you're able to decide (it won't be easy), take it through to the end, and the results could be remarkable.

### PISCES

This team could end up being one-sided unless you're careful. It will be tempting for Pisces to retreat and let you take the lead, but you'll get a better outcome with the fish's creative input. Having clearly identified roles and regular meetings will help maintain the balance.

## STERLING CHILDREN'S BOOKS

New York

An Imprint of Sterling Publishing Co., Inc.
1166 Avenue of the Americas
New York, NY 10036

© 2019 Guild of Master Craftsman Publications Ltd

ISBN 978-1-4549-3962-7

Distributed in Canada by Sterling Publishing Co., Inc.
c/o Canadian Manda Group, 664 Annette Street
Toronto, Ontario M6S 2C8, Canada

For information about custom editions, special sales, and premium and corporate
purchases, please contact Sterling Special Sales at 800-805-5489
or specialsales@sterlingpublishing.com.

Manufactured in China
Lot #:
2 4 6 8 10 9 7 5 3 1
08/19

sterlingpublishing.com

Design by Jo Chapman
Illustrations by Sara Thielker